#2  Catacombs Mysteries©

To Patrick & Thomas

The Vanishing Act

Happy Reading!

Mary Litton

*Mary Litton*

To David

www.MaryLitton.com

Editor:  Jack Bradford
Interior Director:  Elizabeth Clare
ISBN:  0615699529
ISBN-13:  978-0615699523

# CONTENTS

## THE MAGIC ACT

Colorful fall leaves decorated the grounds surrounding the stone buildings of St. John's Church.  Inside, the youth group was putting on a talent show in the Fellowship Hall to raise money for new playground equipment.

Will sat in a folding chair with his third-grade Sunday School class, waiting for his turn to go on stage.

He was dressed in black pants and a white button-down shirt. He had tied the cape from his Halloween vampire costume around his neck, and his dad had helped him slick back his brown hair with gel. He looked and felt like a real magician.

He and his partner Hannah had been practicing all week, and they were excited. They had a good act. Will had barely been able to believe his luck when Hannah told him that her dad was a birthday party magician. So, Will had gone over to her house the week before to learn a few tricks. Will was most excited about the grand finale, where he would get inside a large wooden box called a "vanishing cabinet," and Hannah would make him disappear.

Molly sat a few rows ahead of Will and Hannah with the other second-graders. She had just finished her gymnastics routine and was still dressed in a purple leotard decorated with shiny rhinestones.

Her mother had twisted her hair back into tight braids, tied off with matching purple ribbons. She wore a thin necklace with a small golden cross around her neck. It was the cross Angie had given to her and Will when they discovered the time portal in the basement of St. John's.

Will rubbed the cross in his pocket while waiting to go onstage. He was having a hard time sitting still watching the Terrible Thompson Twins' karate act, until Timmy accidentally punched Tommy in the kneecap. When Tommy put Timmy in a headlock, Father Dan ran out on stage and announced the end of their act.

Next on stage were Katie and her talking pet parakeet, Skeeter. Gingerly, she walked out with Skeeter balanced on the side of her pointed finger. He perched there nervously, looking around from side to side.

"Hello, Skeeter," Katie said to the bird.

"Hello, Beautiful," the bird replied. Skeeter seemed nervous as it began hopping from one foot to the other.

"Skeeter, what is your favorite movie?" Katie asked, stroking its feathers to try to calm it down.

"Parrots of the Caribbean," the bird replied. The audience laughed at the joke, making Skeeter jump and suddenly take flight.

"AAAAAH!" Katie took off running after her pet. Skeeter swooped to the side of the stage where Mrs. Smotherly was standing.

Mrs. Smotherly froze as the bird dove right for her and landed in the middle of her puffy gray hair.

"Help!" Mrs. Smotherly cried, swatting at her hair to try to get Skeeter out, but he was trapped in a web of sticky hairspray.

"Don't hurt him!" cried Katie.

Father Dan ran over with a paper bag, waving it at Mrs. Smotherly's head. Every time he hit her with the bag, Skeeter flapped his wings wildly, trying to get unstuck, causing Mrs. Smotherly to scream and run even faster.

Suddenly, Father Dan leapt forward and bagged Mrs. Smotherly's entire head – hair, forehead, glasses, and all. When Father Dan peeled back the bag, Skeeter was safely captured.

The audience clapped as he returned Skeeter to his cage and quickly shut the door.

Mrs. Smotherly tried to smooth down her hair, which was now a tangled mess, sticking out in all directions. She straightened her crooked glasses as she breathlessly announced, "Up next – Will and Hannah's magic act."

Will felt a flutter in his stomach as he walked up to the stage and looked out at all of the people in the audience. Suddenly he felt very nervous.

*What if I can't remember my lines?* he thought, and his breath caught in his throat. He looked over at Hannah setting up a small table with their tricks, just like they had practiced. Still feeling jittery, Will helped arrange his props. When they were ready, he turned to face the crowd. He held his breath and for a brief second, his mind went blank. His hands clenched into fists and his heart raced.

Everyone in the Fellowship Hall watched him, waiting for him to say something.

Will closed his eyes and took a deep breath. "Welcome," he said nervously, "to the Will and Hannah Magic Show."

He looked out and saw his friends smiling. Suddenly he didn't feel as nervous. He walked over to the table and performed his first trick, pulling a stuffed rabbit out of his magician's hat. The audience clapped. Will exhaled with relief and realized that he was actually enjoying himself.

Next, Hannah made a paper flower wilt and grow on command, and then made it do a little dance that had the audience laughing and clapping.

Molly was watching her friends closely, enjoying the magic, when suddenly her cross grew warm around her neck. She looked around the room for any signs of Angie, but she did not see her. The cross grew warmer, and Molly knew something was wrong.

She stood up and tried not to block anyone's view as she stumbled across the row of shoes to get to the side aisle. She wanted to be ready as soon as Will came off the stage. If Angie needed them at the time portal, they had to get down there together so they could pull the light switch at the same time.

She looked up and saw Will and Hannah pushing a tall wooden box onto the stage.

"For the grand finale," Hannah announced, "I will make Will disappear!"

The audience murmured in excitement.

Molly had a strange feeling.

Hannah opened the door to the cabinet, and Will stepped inside. Molly's cross pulsed with heat.

"And now, with a wave of my magic wand, I will make Will vanish into thin air," Hannah announced. She closed the door on Will and then circled the wand in the air dramatically before tapping on the door three times.

The audience was silent. Hannah smiled and yanked open the door.

The cabinet was empty.

The audience gasped. They jumped to their feet, clapping. Suddenly, Molly knew exactly what she needed to do. She took off running for the basement.

## 2

---

## DISAPPEARING

Will stepped out of the secret door in the back of the vanishing cabinet so that he could hide onstage while Hannah opened the empty box. However, when he stepped out, it did not look like the back of the stage, and he did not hear the audience or Hannah.

As he looked around, he realized that he was in a completely unfamiliar place. He strained his eyes to see in the darkness. He saw tall shelves holding plastic containers and a stack of boxes. His heart raced as he discovered he was in some sort of storage room. Realizing that he needed to get out of this strange room quickly, he turned around to go back into the box, but his breath caught.

The box was no longer there. It had disappeared.

Suddenly, he let out a yelp when he saw something moving in the corner of the room. An overhead light flicked on, and Angie smiled at him.

Will exhaled with relief.

Angie was dressed in the same brown pants and white button-down shirt as she had been before. Her dark curls were pulled back into a ponytail, and her eyes were a warm, welcoming brown.

"Surprise!" she said.

Will felt an immediate sense of calm wash over him when she smiled at him. "Did you make me disappear for real?"

Angie laughed. "I had a little help," she said, pointing to the ceiling. "This magic thing is pretty fun! You should hear them applauding! I'd say you are the best act of the show!"

Will smiled with pride. He couldn't wait to hear what everyone was saying.

Suddenly he remembered something. He stuck his hand in his pocket and pulled out a white packet. "I got this for you," he said, handing it to her.

"Big League Chew!" Angie exclaimed. "My favorite!" She opened up the package and pulled out a large chunk of shredded pink bubble gum. "I'm sorry I interrupted your show," Angie mumbled through a mouth full of gum, "but we didn't have time to wait." Her expression became serious, and for the first time, Will noticed that the cross in his pocket was warm.

"Did someone get into the time portal and change a Bible story?"

Angie nodded.

"What about Molly?"

"She's on her way down," Angie said.

"By herself?" asked Will.

"She can do it," Angie grinned. "She may not know it yet, but she can do it."

3

## THE JOURNEY DOWNSTAIRS

When Molly reached the stairs that led to the basement, or the 'catacombs,' as Father Dan called it, her brain suddenly caught up with her. "Wait," she thought. "I don't have a flashlight or a map." She turned around to go back, but the cross grew even warmer. She knew she did not have time to track down Father Dan and explain why she needed a map of the church and a flashlight.

Her knees shook as she made her way down the stairwell to the basement. With every step, it got cooler and darker. She clutched the handrail and wished she felt as brave as she had upstairs in the light hallway.

When she stepped out onto the basement floor, she blinked as her eyes adjusted. She could only see a couple of feet in front of her before everything turned pitch black. She clutched at the warm cross on her necklace and noticed that it was glowing with light. She unclasped it and held it in front of her. It gave off a faint light, just enough so she could see a little bit ahead.

"Dear God, please help me remember the way," she said quickly as she started down the dark hallway, straining to see ahead.

She pictured the map in her mind. "Left," she whispered to herself at the first corner.  She used her hands to feel her way around the turn.  The hallway grew darker as she moved farther from the light of the stairs.  Her heart beat faster as she gripped the cross in front of her.

Doubt crept into her mind.  "What if I'm wrong and I get lost down here?" Molly wondered.  Suddenly she felt very turned around; she didn't know which way was left or right.

"I can do this," she told herself, feeling her way down the hallway.  Then she came to a corner and could not remember if she should turn left or go straight.

She started to panic. "I'm going to be like one of those kids who get lost in the woods for days, only I don't have wood for a fire or berries to eat," she thought.

She stood frozen with indecision.  She looked around wildly but had no idea where she was.  Her heartbeat thudded in her ears.  "Hug a tree!" she thought.

"That's what you're supposed to do if you
get lost in the woods so that a search party
can come find you!" Molly threw her arms
up on the concrete wall and pressed

herself against it.

"I'm hugging a tree!" she yelled into the darkness. "Search party, if you can hear me, I'm hugging a tree!"

Suddenly the heat from her cross was too much for her skin. "Ouch!" she cried, throwing it from hand to hand, like a game of hot potato.

She suddenly remembered that she needed to turn left.

She exhaled loudly and started moving again. "Thanks, God," she whispered.

She turned left and breathed a sigh of relief when she recognized the long hallway with a small door handle in the middle. She pushed on the handle and opened the door to Room 3C.

Immediately she saw Angie talking to Will.

"I made it!" Molly grinned, so happy to see people again.

"You did it by yourself," Angie said, smiling proudly at her friend.

"That was way too scary alone," Molly said.

"I knew you could do it," Angie said.

Molly looked at Will. "I knew you really disappeared!"

"I took the easy way." Will smirked. "But that's cool that you found your way down here without the map." Molly could tell by his tone that he was really impressed.

"It was no big deal," she replied, choosing to forget her tree-hugging meltdown.

Angie held up a finger, signaling them to wait. She then held it up to her earpiece. "Uh huh, yes, Sir," she said.

"They are here. Now? Yes, Sir, they are on their way."

Angie's smile was replaced by a look of worry as she dropped her finger and looked back at them.

"You have to hurry," Angie said, walking over the pull chain. "Remember, you have to repeat the verse and pull the chain together."

"What is the verse?" Will asked, walking over to put his hand on the chain.

"Ecclesiastes 4:9 'Two people are better than one. They can help each other in everything they do.'"

"You hear that, Will," Molly said, grabbing the chain. "You're better with me than without. Remember that the next time you disappear down here without me!"

"Do you know where we're going?" Will asked Angie.

Angie shook her head. "Only you and God will know. But remember that God is looking out for you, and he will provide you with what you need."

"I'm ready," Molly said, clutching her gold cross. Will pulled his cross out of his pocket.

They looked at each other and nodded.

"*Two people are better than one. They can help each other in everything they do!*" they repeated together, pulling the chain at the same time.

# 4

## POCKET GADGETS

As they pulled the chain, a bright light filled the room. Molly tucked her head into her shoulder and Will covered his eyes with his elbow. They felt a strong wind swirl inside the room. They both tightened their grips on the chain just as the wind whooshed with such force that they felt their feet leave the ground. Will inhaled sharply as his stomach flipped at the sudden movement. Molly held her breath and tried not to scream.

Suddenly everything was still. The light vanished, and they uncovered their eyes. They were standing on top of a hill overlooking the banks of a large, rushing river. They were surrounded by a thick clump of cypress trees and overgrown bushes. The river below was wide and dark, and the water was moving fast.

"We made it," Will said with relief, looking around at what used to be their church basement. His eyes grew big when spotted the large river below them. "That river is huge."

"I hope God gave us floaties," Molly said, looking down at the swift rapids.

"What tools did we get?" Will asked, patting his pockets. He felt something long and narrow, like a stick. He pulled it out and examined it. It was hollow in the middle, so he could see through it. "Is it like a telescope?" he asked, holding it up to one eye.

Molly giggled. "That's not a telescope." She grabbed it and looked it over. "It's a flute," she decided.

Will gave her a doubtful look. "Why would we need a flute?"

Molly's face lit up as she realized the answer. "Because it's a super secret Ninja flute and when you play it, it makes a really high pitched sound that is so deafening, it will bring people to their knees begging you to stop playing!"

Will cocked his head to the side and raised an eyebrow. "A Ninja flute?"

Molly brought it up to her mouth. "Cover your ears, Will. This could hurt."

Will rolled his eyes, but he covered his ears, just in case.

Molly took a deep breath and blew into the flute. Nothing but air came out the other end.

Will shook his head and took the stick back from her. "Hold on," he said, reaching into his other pocket. "What are these?" He pulled out a handful of small, round rocks.

They looked at each other and grinned. "Ammo!" Molly exclaimed.

"It's a pea shooter!" Will said, loading a rock into the tube. Just like a spitball through a straw, he blew one short, strong breath into the shooter and launched the rock over the cliff and down toward the water.

"What did you get?" Will asked, loading up more rocks and firing them out into the trees.

"I hope it isn't another vegetable," Molly said, remembering that her secret weapon last time had been a handful of carrots. Molly reached for her pockets, but stopped short. Her face turned into a frown.

"What's wrong?" Will asked.

"I don't have any pockets in my leotard," Molly answered.

"That's okay," Will said. "I have plenty of rocks to share."

Molly's shoulders fell with disappointment. She kicked at the grass and turned toward the river, trying to hide her tears.

"Molly!" Will cried. "On your back! It's awesome!"

Molly craned her neck to look over her shoulder, but she couldn't see her back. The more she looked, the more she turned. Soon, she was chasing her back like a dog chased its tail.

"Stop!" Will laughed. He reached out and pulled something off and handed it to her. Her eyes grew as she gasped. It was a crossbow, but instead of having an arrow, it was loaded with a three-pronged hook.

"What is it?" she asked in a whisper.

"It's a grappling hook," Will grinned. "My Batman toy used to have one. It shoots out the claw, and it hooks onto something far away. Batman uses it to fly between buildings." Will couldn't believe he was looking at a real one.

Suddenly they heard shouting and a baby crying. They crouched behind the shrubs and looked down by the riverbank, where two women were shouting and calling to something in the water. A group of large boulders stood in the middle of the river, creating small rapids. As they strained their eyes, they saw a basket stuck in the rapids behind one of the boulders.

"Is that basket crying?" Molly asked.

"It sounds like there's a baby in it," Will answered, stretching his neck to try to see inside the basket.

The two women continued to shout and cry at the basket.

"Why would there be a baby in a basket?" Molly asked. Then their jaws dropped open and they looked at each other. "Moses!" they shouted at the same time.

# 5

## ROLL WITH IT

"Double jinx black out!" Molly shouted.

"Not now," Will snapped, mad that he did not jinx Molly first.

Molly shook her finger. "Will, you can't talk until I say your name three times."

"When you time travel, you have to play by current day rules. In Moses's time, you probably only had to say my name once, which you just did. So I'm free!"

Molly narrowed her eyes at Will as she thought about time travel rules for jinx. She shrugged. "Fine. But you owe me a coke when we get back."

Another cry made them look back down toward the basket stuck in the water.

"This must be the Nile River," Molly said. "It's the longest river in the world!"

"That means we're in Egypt!" Will exclaimed. "I've always wanted to go to Egypt! This is where people built the first city ever in history. They settled here because the Nile River creates good dirt for farming in the middle of the desert. They had pharaohs, pyramids and mummies!"

"Mummies?" Molly asked. "As in werewolves, monsters and mummies?"

"Not scary Halloween mummies," Will said. "They discovered a special way to preserve the bodies of the people who died so that they would always look the same," Will explained. "In real life, mummies aren't scary; they are a neat way to see what people looked like a long time ago."

"Well, the only 'mummy' I want to see is the one who belongs to this baby." Molly smiled at her joke while Will rolled his eyes.

"According to the story, she should be nearby," Will said.

"Yeah," Molly said, remembering the story. "When Moses was born, the Hebrews were slaves. The king was worried that the slaves would start an army and rebel, so he ordered that all Hebrew baby boys be killed so they wouldn't be able to create an army when they grew up."

"Moses was Hebrew, but his mother wanted to protect him," Will added, thinking of the Sunday School lesson. "So she put him in a basket and hid him in the reeds of the river."

"That must be her!" Molly exclaimed, looking down at the crying women. "But remember, they have a happy ending because the king's daughter will find Moses and decide to keep him and raise him like her own son."

"If that's his mom, then who is the other woman?" Will asked.

"His sister," Molly said. "Remember? She hides to watch what happens, and when she sees the princess take him, she offers to find a Hebrew nanny for him."

"That was really smart," Will said. "That way his mom was able to teach him all of the Hebrew stories and all about his people, so that when he is a prince, he fights to free the Hebrews from slavery."

"These women saved his life," Molly said softly. "And I don't even know their names."

"The basket was supposed to be in the reeds where the princess will find it," Will said. "If it's not in the reeds, the princess won't see it."

"Someone must have pushed it into the river," Molly said.

They saw something moving in the distance. "Oh, no," Molly grabbed onto Will's sleeve. "The princess is on her way to bathe!"

Will looked down at the procession walking toward the river. "Our mission must be to get the basket into the reeds."

"We don't have much time," Molly said. Looking down, she saw that they were perched on top of a steep cliff with no path down to the riverbank.

"How do we get down?" Will asked.

Molly grinned. "How do you think we get down a hill? We have to roll!"

Will looked down the rocky cliff anxiously and shook his head. "It's too steep. We should try to hike down," he said.

"No way, we'll fall. Plus, we don't have time," Molly said.

Will took a timid step, and his foot held firmly on the ground. "No," he said, taking another step. "It's fine." Feeling more confident, he walked another few steps, but his foot suddenly slid out from under him, sending him flying on to the ground with a loud *whump*. Rocks tumbled below him, gaining speed until they turned into a small rock slide.

Will immediately changed his mind and lay down next to Molly.

As they started to roll, it was slow and a little fun, but quickly they began gaining speed, flipping over so fast that their bodies were lifting off the ground. They landed with such force that it knocked the wind out of them. Their arms and legs began to flail out around them, turning them into human windmills.

Abruptly, Will hit something soft with great force. He rolled over the object and landed on top of it, completely stopping his roll.

So happy to have survived, he lay on top of the soft mound, catching his breath and thanking God. But then the mound began to move. He jumped up and looked down to see that the heap that had stopped his fall was Molly.

"Molly!" he cried, frantically trying to flip her over. "Are you okay?"

Molly's whole body shook as Will tried to roll her.

"Are you hurt?" Will cried. He uncovered her head and looked down at her red face, streaked with tears.

A huge grin spread across Molly's face, and he realized that she was shaking with laughter. "That was so fun!" Molly cried.

"That was not fun," Will said, pulling her up to her feet. His legs were still shaking.

Molly stopped laughing to look at him. "Then why are you smiling?" she asked.

Will realized that he was grinning. "I'm just happy to be alive," he said.

Suddenly they heard a scream. They turned and saw that Moses's basket had been sucked farther into the current and was now perched between two rocks, right over a small waterfall.

At any second, the basket could tip over and Moses would be thrown into the river.

"Let's go," Will said. "We have to save Moses and the Hebrews."

6

## CREATIVE FRIENDS

Will and Molly walked over to the crying women.  As they approached, the women looked around suspiciously.  "Who are you?" asked the sister, stepping in front of her mother.

"Don't be afraid," Molly said.  "God sent us to help you save your baby."

"God sent you?" Moses's mother asked.

"Your baby is very important, and we're going to get him out of the river," Will said.

"I can't let them hurt him," his mother said as tears pooled in her eyes.

"He'll be safe if we can get him into the reeds," Will said. "God will watch after him."

The mother cried in relief.

"I'm Molly, and this is Will," Molly said.

"I am Jochebed," Moses's mother said. "And this is my daughter, Miriam."

"It is really nice to know your names," Molly said. "How did you make such a strong basket?"

"I used a basket made of papyrus and then coated it in tar so that it would float," Jochebed answered.

"That's really creative," Molly said, impressed.

"Then we put it in the reeds and went to hide, but when we looked back, the basket had come out of the reeds and was stuck up the river in those rocks," Miriam said. "Are you going to swim out to get him?"

"That current is too strong for swimming – we'd get swept away," Will replied. "We need something to help us float."

"We need a raft," Molly said.

"How are we going to find a raft?" Will asked.

"Will, we are talking to the inventors of one of the most famous rafts in history." Molly said, turning to Jochebed and Miriam. "Can you help us make a raft?"

Will nodded. "I guess if the verse tells us *two people are better than one*, imagine what four people can do if they work together.

"I think they could save a baby trapped in a river," Molly answered.

## 7

## THE NILE CROCODILE

Jochebed and Miriam ran into the woods to gather long branches. They used reeds to tie them together into a small raft.

"This looks pretty good," Molly said. "Let's give it a try."

"We'll need to launch the raft upstream so that we aren't fighting the current," Will said.

Molly looked up the river bank. "Up there," she said, pointing to a small sandy beach that jutted out into the river.

They each picked up a side of the raft and started toward the launch site. Suddenly, Molly stopped moving. She froze like a statue. Her mouth gaped open.

"Come on, Molly," Will said, tugging his side of the raft. "We don't have much time."

Will heard a loud hiss that made the hair on his neck stand up. He looked ahead and saw a huge crocodile blocking their way to the river. It was nearly sixteen feet long and probably weighed five hundred pounds. Will recognized it instantly.

"It's a Nile crocodile," Will whispered. "I saw one of these at an animal assembly at school. They eat everything, including people."

"It looks really hungry," Molly whimpered.

The crocodile lunged forward and hissed.  Will and Molly jumped back, trembling.

"What else did you learn about these monsters?" Molly asked, her voice cracked with fear.

"They are really caring parents," Will said shakily.  "The mom and dad guard their eggs until they hatch."

"That's great, Will," Molly said sarcastically.  "That'll make me feel much better about him when he's eating me for breakfast!"

The crocodile opened its large mouth and showed rows of sharp, terrifying teeth.

"I've heard that crocodiles can't go sideways, so you're supposed to run in a zigzag motion," Molly said.

"Its eyes!" Will said excitedly, remembering another fact from his assembly. "They're the most vulnerable part. We have to hit it in the eyes!"

"The pea shooter!" Molly exclaimed too loudly, causing the crocodile to hiss again

Will slowly reached into his pocket and pulled out the long stick and a handful of rocks. "What if I miss and make it mad?"

"Then we'll just zigzag run away," Molly said. "Come on, this is our only chance."

Will's hands trembled as he loaded the rocks into the shooter.

"Aim carefully," Molly whispered. The crocodile hissed and Will's hands fumbled as he dropped the rocks. The crocodile lunged toward them again, and Will and Molly jumped back.

Will grabbed another handful and loaded it up. "Why didn't you get the pea shooter?  I have terrible aim."

He held the shooter up to his mouth and aimed.

"You have to get closer," Molly whispered.  "You're not close enough to hurt it, it'll just get it mad."

"I don't want to get any closer," Will said.  Molly tucked in behind Will and shoved him hard in the back.  "Stop it, Molly," Will pushed back as she continued to shove him closer.

The crocodile hissed, Will aimed the pea shooter, and Molly braced herself behind Will.  "Shoot!" she called, just as the crocodile lunged even closer.

Will took a big breath and blew out with all his might.  A rock flew through the air and hit the crocodile right in the middle of the forehead.

The crocodile growled and hissed.  It was mad.  Suddenly, its legs started moving rapidly as it came at them.

"Again!" Molly screamed.

Will brought up the shooter and shot again. This time the rock hit the crocodile right in the eye. The crocodile froze like it was confused.

Will launched a third rock and hit the other eye. The crocodile made a whimpering noise and turned to retreat into the tree line.

"Great aim!" Molly said, clapping Will on the back.

He heaved a huge sigh of relief. His hands were still shaking as he put the pea shooter back in his pants. "I just fought off a crocodile!"

"Wait 'til I tell everyone at school about this!" Molly said.

Will grinned. He couldn't wait for Molly to tell everyone at school.

## 8

---

## THE WILD RIVER

"Come on, we have to get Moses before the basket tips over," Molly said, grabbing her side of the raft.

They waded into the water until they was standing knee-deep. They kept a tight grip on the raft to stop it from being swept down the river in the fast-flowing current.

"Ready?" asked Will.

Molly swallowed hard and nodded.

"Now!" they yelled, and pushed the raft into the current. The raft teetered dangerously close to tipping over while they slid on to their bellies like a boogie board. Once they found their balance, they realized they were going much faster than they had expected.

"We're going too fast!" Molly cried. Will could barely hear her over the sound of the rushing water. They kicked with all of their strength, but they couldn't steer the raft toward the rocks.

"We're going to miss it!" Will yelled. "We need your grappling hook!"

Molly struggled to keep her grip on the raft as she reached onto her back, nearly tipping them into the water. Will held the raft steady as she aimed the hook in front of her.

"Shoot it at the rocks and we'll use it to pull ourselves in," Will shouted.

Molly pointed the bow at the rocks. With a slight pull of the trigger, the claw released with mighty force, whizzing through the air with a rope attached. It hit the rock so hard that it wrapped around itself several times, creating a taut line and causing the raft to suddenly buck to a stop.

"It's too strong," she cried, "I have to let go of the raft!"

"NO!" Will called. "I'll lose you!"

"Hold on to me!" Molly yelled, struggling to keep her grip on the grappling hook line as the strong current pulled at the raft.

Will threw his arms around Molly's neck piggyback style and let go of the raft. The raft flipped and turned as it disappeared down the river. Molly kept both hands on the gun tethered to the boulder.

Struggling to keep their heads above water, they kicked with great force as Molly pulled her way up the rope, hand over hand, until they made their way toward the rapids.

Waves crashed over them as they finally got to Moses. They gulped for air as they held on to the boulders.

"Grab the basket," Molly shouted. "I see the princess getting close to the river!"

Will kept one arm around Molly's neck and used the other hand to pull the basket out of the rocks.

For a moment, Moses stopped crying and looked up at them through the slits in the basket. He was so little and cute – it was hard to picture him as a man parting the Red Sea with his staff. Molly and Will smiled as they looked down at one of history's greatest leaders.

"Hi, Moses," Molly whispered. "You have quite an adventure ahead of you."

"It's hard to imagine that this baby is going to lead the Hebrews out of slavery and to the promised land of Israel," Will said.

"He's also going to give us parts of the Bible like the Ten Commandments," Molly added.

"We have to get him to safety. If we didn't have the Ten Commandments, think of how bad the world would be."

Molly shuddered at the thought of a world full of liars, thieves and murderers.

"If we push it off to the side, the current should take it right into those reeds faster than we can swim," Will said.

"Are you sure?" Molly asked, looking at tiny baby Moses in the basket. He looked so fragile and Molly understood what an important leader he would become.

"It's the only way," Will said, nodding toward the river banks where the princess and her attendants were closing in on the river. "God will protect him."

They pushed the basket out of the rapids and back toward the river bank.

They watched nervously as the basket wobbled in the current and then righted itself. It floated down the river toward the tall grass. The basket slowed down and eventually settled in a small nest of reeds just as they saw the princess and her attendants walking up to the river.

Immediately the princess saw the basket. Her assistant waded into the water and grabbed it.

They watched the princess reach into the basket and lift Moses to her chest. Just then, Miriam came out of the trees.

"We did it," Molly smiled, realizing that she was exhausted. She noticed the strength of the current pushing against her. "Will, I don't think I can swim back to the side."

Will looked around and felt frightened. His arms were shaking from fatigue as well – there was no way he could swim back to the banks. They were stuck in the middle of the Nile.  How could they get out?

Suddenly they saw a bright light.  Will and Molly covered their eyes.  A second later, the flash was over and everything was quiet and still.  When they opened their eyes, they were sitting on the floor of the storage room.

## 9

## THE WAY BACK

"We're back," Molly said gratefully, falling back on the ground.

Will collapsed on the floor beside her. "I've never been so tired in my life."

Angie stood over them, looking concerned. "Are you two okay?" she asked.

"We fought a crocodile." Will said matter-of-factly.

"And swam the Nile River," Molly added.

"You did a great job. God is very pleased," she said. "You should probably hurry. The crowd is getting worried that you really disappeared. Hannah has tried to open the door twice now."

"Isn't the show over?" Molly asked. "We've been gone for so long."

Angie shook her head. "When you go through the time portal, time doesn't move here. You get back the same second that you left. So nobody knows that you've been missing."

She offered a hand to pull Molly up. Will took Angie's other hand. She pulled them with such force that they nearly flew up onto their feet.

"Whoa," Molly said. "You angels are strong."

"We have to figure out who is changing these stories," Will said.

"That was really close," Molly agreed. "If they got away with it, think of how different everything would be."

"We should start doing some detective work to figure out who is sneaking into the time portal," Will said.

"That could be really fun," Molly said. "We can wear disguises."

"Yeah," Will agreed, "we could take notes and figure out who may be sneaking down to the basement."

"Does that sound like a good idea, Ang...?" Molly's words trailed off as she realized Angie was no longer in the room.

Molly shook her head. "I don't think I'll ever get used to that."

"Come on," said Will. "Let's get back to the show."

"And tell everyone about your crocodile?" Molly asked with a twinkle in her eye.

"Maybe one day," Will said, grinning, as he pulled open the door. But instead of stepping out into the catacombs hallway, they found themselves squished into a very small, dark space. A door opened in front of them, and they saw the audience gasping at them.

They stepped out of the vanishing cabinet and onto the stage. Hannah's eyes were as wide as moons as she realized she made two people reappear. She smiled and said a triumphant "Ta Dah!"

The entire audience jumped to their feet and clapped and cheered.

Molly and Will looked at each other and grinned. They took a long bow, thinking how nice it was to be appreciated.

# Exodus 1:22 – 2:10 NRSV

Then Pharaoh commanded all his people, 'Every boy that is born to the Hebrews you shall throw into the Nile, but you shall let every girl live.'

Now a man from the house of Levi went and married a Levite woman. The woman conceived and bore a son; and when she saw that he was a fine baby, she hid him for three months. When she could hide him no longer she got a papyrus basket for him, and plastered it with bitumen and pitch; she put the child in it and placed it among the reeds on the bank of the river. His sister stood at a distance, to see what would happen to him.

The daughter of Pharaoh came down to bathe at the river, while her attendants walked beside the river. She saw the basket among the reeds and sent her maid to bring it. When she opened it, she saw the child. He was crying, and she took pity on him. 'This must be one of the Hebrews' children,' she said. Then his sister said to Pharaoh's daughter, 'Shall I go and get you a nurse from the Hebrew women to nurse the child for you?' Pharaoh's daughter said to her, 'Yes.' So the girl went and called the child's mother. Pharaoh's daughter said to her, 'Take this child and nurse it for me, and I will give you your wages.' So the woman took the child and nursed it.

When the child grew up, she brought him to Pharaoh's daughter, and she took him as her son. She named him Moses, 'because', she said, 'I drew him out of the water.'

# ACKNOWLEDGMENTS

I would like to thank all of my wonderful readers who continue to encourage and support me. Watching your faces light up when you read my books make it all worthwhile! A special thanks to Jodah, Matthew, Elizabeth, Maisie, Max and Owen. Thank you to the Altenburger Publicity Team for the strategy sessions. Thank you to my impromptu sales team including Art and Jenny Fowler, Shannon and Todd Akers, Clarke and Joe Harrison, Gourmet Incorporated, Inc., and Around the Block Books. Thank you to Yellowmane for a great web site and all of your support – technical and otherwise. Thank you to Joylyn Hannahs for the fabulous author photos – you do amazing work! Finally, thank you to clergy and members of St. James Episcopal Church for scholarly advice and loving support.

DON'T MISS WILL AND MOLLY'S OTHER
CATACOMBS MYSTERIES© ADVENTURES!

#1  Secret of the Catacombs

#2  The Vanishing Act

#3  Beginning of the End

To learn more about The Catacombs Mysteries© series
and order your next book, visit the author's web site:

**www.MaryLitton.com**

# ABOUT THE AUTHOR

© Joylyn Hannahs

Mary Litton has lived in the DC area for over 12 years. When she was a girl, her goal was to be a published author by the age of ten. Even though it took a little longer than she expected, she thinks the Catacombs Mysteries© series was worth the wait! She is happily married and the proud mom of two children and one chocolate lab.

Made in the USA
Charleston, SC
08 December 2012